It Was Like a Fairy Tale!

Elizabeth could hardly catch her breath. A real, live prince—sitting across the table from her, sipping a chocolate shake just like an ordinary person!

Arthur leaned forward, looking earnestly into her eyes. "Elizabeth, I've dreamed my whole life about seeing how other children live. Here, nobody knows who I am. As far as they're concerned, I'm just a regular boy visiting another country for the first time. Please, will you help me keep my secret?"

Bantam Books in the SWEET VALLEY TWINS AND FRIENDS series
Ask your bookseller for the books you have missed

#1 BEST FRIENDS
#2 TEACHER'S PET
#3 THE HAUNTED HOUSE
#4 CHOOSING SIDES
#5 SNEAKING OUT
#6 THE NEW GIRL
#7 THREE'S A CROWD
#8 FIRST PLACE
#9 AGAINST THE RULES
#10 ONE OF THE GANG
#11 BURIED TREASURE
#12 KEEPING SECRETS
#13 STRETCHING THE TRUTH
#14 TUG OF WAR
#15 THE OLDER BOY
#16 SECOND BEST
#17 BOYS AGAINST GIRLS
#18 CENTER OF ATTENTION
#19 THE BULLY
#20 PLAYING HOOKY
#21 LEFT BEHIND
#22 OUT OF PLACE
#23 CLAIM TO FAME
#24 JUMPING TO CONCLUSIONS
#25 STANDING OUT
#26 TAKING CHARGE
#27 TEAMWORK
#28 APRIL FOOL!
#29 JESSICA AND THE BRAT ATTACK

#30 PRINCESS ELIZABETH
#31 JESSICA'S BAD IDEA
#32 JESSICA ON STAGE
#33 ELIZABETH'S NEW HERO
#34 JESSICA, THE ROCK STAR
#35 AMY'S PEN PAL
#36 MARY IS MISSING
#37 THE WAR BETWEEN THE TWINS
#38 LOIS STRIKES BACK
#39 JESSICA AND THE MONEY MIX-UP
#40 DANNY MEANS TROUBLE
#41 THE TWINS GET CAUGHT
#42 JESSICA'S SECRET
#43 ELIZABETH'S FIRST KISS
#44 AMY MOVES IN
#45 LUCY TAKES THE REINS
#46 MADEMOISELLE JESSICA
#47 JESSICA'S NEW LOOK
#48 MANDY MILLER FIGHTS BACK
#49 THE TWINS' LITTLE SISTER
#50 JESSICA AND THE SECRET STAR
#51 ELIZABETH THE IMPOSSIBLE

Sweet Valley Twins Super Editions
#1 THE CLASS TRIP
#2 HOLIDAY MISCHIEF
#3 THE BIG CAMP SECRET

Sweet Valley Twins Super Chiller Editions
#1 THE CHRISTMAS GHOST
#2 THE GHOST IN THE GRAVEYARD
#3 THE CARNIVAL GHOST

SWEET VALLEY TWINS
AND FRIENDS

Princess
Elizabeth

Written by
Jamie Suzanne

Created by
FRANCINE PASCAL

A BANTAM SKYLARK BOOK®
NEW YORK · TORONTO · LONDON · SYDNEY · AUCKLAND

RL 4, 008-012

PRINCESS ELIZABETH
A Bantam Skylark Book / June 1989

ISBN 0-553-15715-9

Published simultaneously in the United States and Canada

PRINTED IN THE UNITED STATES OF AMERICA

OPM   10 9 8 7 6 5 4 3

Princess
Elizabeth

One

◇

"Living in Santa Dora must be just like living a real-life fairy tale," Jessica Wakefield said with a sigh. She was lying on her twin's bed, leafing through the pages of the book Elizabeth had brought home from the library. She held up a picture of a king and queen. "Imagine living in a country that still has royalty!"

Elizabeth couldn't help teasing her sister just a little. "I thought you weren't very excited about studying Santa Dora for the next two weeks," she said, laughing. "In fact, I can even quote you. 'Who cares about such a dinky little country—it's not famous for anything.' "

Jessica tossed back her long blond hair and grinned at her sister. "You're right," she admitted, dropping the book and sitting up straight. "I wasn't too interested in Santa Dora. But that was before I found out that Arthur Castle would be coming as an exchange student." She picked up the book again, flipping a page. "I wonder if he'll be as good-looking as the boys in these pictures," she mused. "They all have gorgeous dark, curly hair and such beautiful olive skin."

Elizabeth looked up from the map she was drawing. "Well," she observed pragmatically, "you don't have long to wonder. He'll be here tomorrow."

"I know," Jessica sighed. "Oh, Lizzie, I just can't *wait* until tomorrow morning. The Unicorns have painted this terrific 'Welcome, Arthur' banner to hang up at school. And we made a huge batch of Santa Doran pastries for everybody in homeroom, with raisins and almonds in them. Arthur will *love* them."

Elizabeth laughed again. Arthur Castle was coming all the way from Santa Dora to stay in Sweet Valley for two weeks while his parents were in Los Angeles on business, and during Arthur's visit, the sixth graders would be studying his country. Every student was working on a project that had a Santa Doran theme. Some of the kids had even decided to get together and do something extra, like the welcome Jessica and the Unicorns were planning for the next morning.

Elizabeth gave her sister a glance. "How's your project coming, Jess?" she asked.

"Oh, just fine," Jessica said breezily. She had chosen to do an oral report instead of a written one. She looked down at the library book. "Uh, would you mind if I borrowed your book, Liz? It's got some stuff on the royal family I could use."

"Sure," Elizabeth said with a grin, going back to her map. "Just be sure I get it back. OK?"

Although Elizabeth and Jessica were identical twins, with the same long blond hair, cute dimples, and blue-green eyes—they were about as different as any two sisters could be. More than anything, Jessica liked to spend time with her friends in the Unicorns, an exclusive club whose members were the prettiest and most popular girls at Sweet Valley Middle School. They spent a lot of time talking about clothes, movies, and boys, and loved to share the latest gossip. Elizabeth enjoyed spending time with her friends, too, but she also liked to have time to herself for reading and thinking. She was a good organizer and her friends always looked on her as a leader.

The projects the two girls had chosen told a lot about their differences. Elizabeth, who loved learning about new places, was making a map of Santa Dora, a tiny kingdom on the beautiful Mediterranean seacoast between southern France and northern Spain. In addition to drawing the map, she was writing a report on Santa Dora's history for the class newspaper, *The Sweet Valley Sixers*. Elizabeth's biggest dream was to become a writer someday.

Jessica, on the other hand, thought that doing something as major as a map *and* a written report was much too much work. But as soon as she discovered Santa Dora was still governed by a king and queen, she decided it was worth doing an oral report on the royal family. She couldn't wait for Arthur to tell her everything he knew about the king and queen. That would certainly be a lot quicker than spending hours cooped up in a stuffy old library. And, she would enjoy spending time with a handsome, curly haired boy.

"Girls," Mrs. Wakefield called from downstairs, "it's time to set the table for dinner. Whose turn is it tonight?"

"Mine, Mom," Elizabeth replied, raising her voice. "I'll be right there."

Jessica groaned. "Darn," she said, making a face. "That means I'm supposed to clean up the kitchen tonight, and I've got to be at Ellen's house by seven. The Unicorns are meeting to put the finishing touches on Arthur's welcome."

Elizabeth stood up and put her map in her notebook, preparing for what she suspected was coming next.

Jessica stood up, too, and cast a hopeful look at her sister. "Lizzie, do you suppose I could get you to trade with me?"

"I traded with you the night before last," Elizabeth pointed out. She gave Jessica a firm look. "Doing the dishes is a lot more work than setting the table, you know."

Jessica smiled. "I know. But you're so *good* at it, Lizzie," she said cajolingly, "and you always make it look so easy." She smiled again. "Pretty-please, big sister? Just one more time? I promise I won't ask again—this week, anyway."

Elizabeth couldn't help laughing at her twin's promise. She *was* Jessica's older sister by four minutes, and sometimes those four minutes seemed more like four years. Although Jessica was good at a lot of things, taking responsibility wasn't one of them.

"And I'll also promise," Jessica added, "to clean up the bathroom."

Elizabeth considered. "Oh, all right," she agreed finally, even though she suspected that Jessica's idea of cleaning up the bathroom meant tossing the dirty towels into the hamper and slamming the lid.

"Oh, *thank* you, Lizzie!" Jessica cried, hugging her twin. She danced down the stairs, calling out, "*I'm* setting the table tonight, Mom!"

"Have you gotten started on your report yet, Jessica?" Mary Wallace asked, as the Unicorns settled down for their meeting.

"Not really," Jessica confided, pulling a book out of her bag. "I'm sort of waiting for Arthur to fill me in on the major stuff. But I did borrow this book from Liz that tells everything about the royal family. Maybe it will give us some ideas for our party. This is actually turning out to be a lot more work than I expected. I hope I get a good grade on it."

Lila Fowler turned to Jessica. "It doesn't sound like very much work to me." She yawned, and made a show of patting her hand over her mouth. "Actually, oral reports are always a little *boring*, don't you think?"

"But royalty isn't the least bit boring," Jessica replied, stung a little by her friend's objection. She flipped open Elizabeth's book to a picture of King Armand II and Queen Stephanie, seated on side-by-side thrones, wearing purple velvet cloaks and diamond-studded crowns. "See? Don't they look *wonderful*?"

Ellen Riteman leaned forward. "Wouldn't you just *love* to be a princess in Santa Dora?" she sighed enviously. "Just think of all the wonderful purple clothes you'd have!" Purple—the color of royalty—was the Unicorns' official club color. They all tried to wear something purple to school every day, so that their classmates would be sure to recognize them as Unicorns.

Mary Wallace studied the picture. "What a great-looking couple," she said. "I'll bet they lead a fairy-tale life."

Jessica got a faraway look in her eyes. "I'll bet they do, too," she agreed. "They probably have servants to wait on them hand and foot." She wrinkled her nose. "If you were a princess, you'd *never* have to do the dishes."

Lila gave the picture a brief glance. "Royalty *is* pretty interesting," she admitted. She tossed her light brown hair back over her shoulders. "You know," she said suddenly, "I think, as Unicorns, that we ought to do something really special for our visitor. After all, *The Sweet Valley Sixers* is coming out with a special edition, and we can't let a newspaper outdo us, can we?"

"You mean, something *more* than our welcome tomorrow morning?" Ellen asked doubtfully.

Jessica frowned. When she'd suggested the idea

of giving Arthur a special welcome, the Unicorns had thought it was great. Now, it seemed, Lila thought it wasn't enough.

"Go ahead, Lila," Jessica said tartly, "why don't you tell us what you have in mind?"

"I'm not exactly sure," Lila said, "but it doesn't seem right to let *The Sixers* steal the spotlight, does it? We need to do something that will really catch everybody's attention."

"But what?" Mary asked. She began to tick people's class projects off on her fingers. "Charlie Cashman and Jerry McAllister have already gotten started on a model of the Chateau Royale, Ken Matthews and Jim Sturbridge are doing a skit on Santa Doran history, Caroline Pearce is giving an oral report on Santa Doran paintings, Brooke Dennis is collecting tapes for a talk on Santa Doran music—"

Jessica's eyes widened as she was suddenly struck by a terrific idea, an idea so absolutely *right* that she knew everyone would love it. "I know!" she cried. "We'll give a *party!*"

Ellen looked at her. "A party?" she echoed doubtfully. "Of course, the Unicorns give wonderful parties, but I don't really see the connection."

"But there *is* a connection!" Jessica insisted. "We'll hold a Santa Doran festival in Arthur's honor, with costumes and music and dancing and plenty of Santa Doran food! And everybody can bring the fun part of their projects. Ken and Jim can do their skit, Caroline can put up her pictures, Brooke can play her tapes, Charlie and Jerry can set up their model—it'll be terrific!"

They all looked at Lila. "Jessica," she said slowly, "I think you might have something there."

"We could have the party on my patio," Ellen offered. "With the right decorations, it could look like a Santa Doran plaza."

"We could get some authentic recipes and do the cooking ourselves," Mary added.

Lila frowned. "I'm sure my father's caterer would be glad to prepare anything we asked him to. That way we wouldn't have to do cleanup."

Jessica clapped her hands ecstatically. "And we could make those beautiful little lace aprons that the girls wear in Santa Dora and weave some ribbons and flowers into our hair! Everybody will *love* it! And Arthur will be impressed out of his mind."

A smile spread slowly over Lila's face. "Jessica," she said, "I have to congratulate you. Your idea is fabulous. Parties are exactly the kind of thing the Unicorns do best. And it's *so* much better than a special edition of the newspaper."

All the Unicorns nodded in agreement. A party was the perfect idea.

"But are you really sure," Elizabeth said slowly, when Jessica finished telling her about the Unicorns' new plan, "that Arthur will be impressed by a Santa Doran festival?"

"Of *course* he'll be impressed!" Jessica exclaimed indignantly. "Why wouldn't he be? When he sees all the decorations and the costumes and hears the music and tastes the food, he'll feel right at home." She frowned at Elizabeth. Why did her sister always throw cold water on her ideas?

Elizabeth looked thoughtful for a moment. "But if I were a kid visiting America for the first time, I'd be pretty interested in what American kids do for fun. Wouldn't you?"

"Well, maybe," Jessica shrugged. "He can do all that, too. But *our* party is going to be something so special that he'll never, ever forget it." She grinned delightedly. "You just wait and see."

Two

◇

"Oh, no!" Amy Sutton groaned as she and Elizabeth walked into the sixth-grade homeroom on Monday morning. Amy was Elizabeth's best friend and today the whole sixth grade was gathering in one special homeroom. "Would you look at that!"

"The thought is nice," Elizabeth said, trying not to giggle, "but I think they've gone a little overboard."

The two girls were looking at a big white sheet that hung across the blackboard. In huge red letters, it said, "Welcome, Arthur!" Beneath that, the greeting was repeated in Spanish. Down at the bottom was a little picture of a Unicorn.

Amy nodded toward the front of the room. "Do

you suppose that's Arthur?" she whispered. "Hey, he's really cute."

Elizabeth looked. "It must be him," she said. A boy she'd never seen before was standing at the front of the classroom talking to Mr. Davis. He had dark curly hair, large dark eyes, and olive skin. She noticed that his jeans and sneakers looked brand-new.

Amy frowned and twisted a wisp of her hair around her finger. "Funny—he doesn't *look* like an exchange student. Isn't that a California Angels T-shirt he's wearing?"

Elizabeth giggled. "What did you expect? Velvet knickers and a ruffled white shirt?"

Amy grinned. "You're right," she said. "I guess they only wear those folk costumes for the tourists, huh?"

"Why don't you ask Arthur?" Elizabeth suggested.

Mr. Davis rapped on his desk for attention. "If you'll take your seats," he called out, "we'll get started. I know you're all anxious to meet our special guest."

They all hurried to their seats and waited expectantly. Standing beside Mr. Davis, Arthur looked around the classroom. Elizabeth noticed how poised and sure of himself he looked, and suspected that he was used to dealing with new situations.

"Class, I'd like you to meet Arthur Castle, from Santa Dora," Mr. Davis said. He put his hand on Arthur's shoulder. "Arthur, may I present to you, the sixth-grade class of Sweet Valley Middle School?" He smiled. "We're very glad to have you with us for the next two weeks. While you're here, we're going to be studying all about your country."

Arthur smiled, showing even white teeth. "I am most honored," he said. His voice was accented and he spoke with a slight formality that sounded strange to Elizabeth's ears, but intriguing. "I am looking forward with great pleasure to learning many new things about the wonderful United States of America."

In the back of the room, there was a rustle as Lila Fowler stood up.

"Now?" Ellen Riteman asked in a loud whisper.

"Now," Lila commanded.

And suddenly, all the Unicorns in the class were out of their seats and running up to the front of the room, where they lined up in a row. While everybody else looked on in surprise, they broke into an ear-splitting cheer, waving their arms and stamping their feet vigorously. "W-E-L-C-O-M-E spells WELCOME," they chanted. "WELCOME, ARTHUR!"

Elizabeth could feel her face flushing red. She

was embarrassed that her twin was up there doing
such a silly cheer, and she was embarrassed for
Arthur, too. He was looking down at his new
sneakers, and she could see that the tips of his
ears were pink.

"And now," Lila Fowler announced, when they
were finished with their cheer, "we have a treat
for everybody, in honor of Arthur." She stepped
forward and whipped a white cloth off a big tray
of strange-looking pastries. "The Unicorns," she
said dramatically, "will now hand out these tradi-
tional Santa Doran raisin-and-almond pastries that
we baked for this occasion." Lila turned around
and presented one to Arthur.

"This is for you, Arthur," she said. "Compli-
ments of the Unicorns."

Mr. Davis cleared his throat. Elizabeth thought
it sounded as if he were strangling a laugh. "Uh,
thank you, Lila," he said hurriedly. "And thank
you, Unicorns."

Arthur bowed from the waist. "Yes," he said,
"*muchas gracias*, many thanks. I am deeply honored by your wonderful welcome." But he almost
choked on his pastry as he took the empty seat in
the row just in front of her.

When Elizabeth bit into her own pastry, she
understood Arthur's reaction. The pastries were

dry and hard. And even though Arthur had impeccable manners and wonderful poise, Elizabeth sensed he didn't like being in the spotlight.

Wrinkling his forehead, Arthur Castle looked down at the science workbook in front of him. Then he looked up at the thermometer on his lab table. They were doing an experiment that involved temperatures. The experiment itself wasn't difficult, but for the life of him, he couldn't figure out the thermometer. It *looked* like the thermometers back home, but the numbers were completely *wrong*. They just didn't make sense. He knew he should raise his hand and ask the teacher, but if he did, everybody would stare at him. And he didn't want to be stared at.

Sensing his confusion, Elizabeth leaned forward and introduced herself and then asked if she could be of any help.

Arthur nodded gratefully. "Thank you, Elizabeth Wakefield," he said. "Perhaps you can." He pointed to the thermometer. "I'm afraid there is something I do not understand. About these numbers, I mean."

"The numbers?" Elizabeth looked at the thermometer. She threw him a questioning look. "But they're the same numbers as always. What is it you don't understand?''

"But here—" He put his finger at the 32-degree mark. "Here it says 'freezing.' In my country, water freezes at zero degrees. And here—" He moved his finger to the 212-degree mark. "Here it says 'boiling.' In Santa Dora, water boils at one hundred degrees." He frowned, shaking his head. "I do not understand how your water and our water can be so different."

Elizabeth stared at the thermometer, and then she began to laugh. For a moment, Arthur thought she was laughing at him, and he shifted uncomfortably in his chair.

"Oh, I'm sorry, Arthur!" she said contritely. "I wasn't laughing at you. I was laughing at—well, at the differences in the way we do things."

"I still do not understand," Arthur said, frowning at her.

"The difference isn't in the water, it's in the *thermometers*," Elizabeth said. She flipped ahead a couple of pages in the workbook, and then showed him a picture. "See? In America, our thermometers work according to the Fahrenheit scale, where water boils at two-hundred-and-twelve degrees and freezes at thirty-two degrees. But it says here that the majority of countries use the Celsius or centigrade scale. On that scale, water boils at one hundred degrees and freezes at zero. I've never thought about it before, but I guess *we're* the ones who are out of step!"

Now it was Arthur's turn to laugh. "Perhaps we can learn from each other," he replied diplomatically.

Elizabeth nodded. "I guess that's the point of exchange programs," she said, considering. "To learn from each other."

Arthur glanced at her admiringly. Elizabeth seemed different than the girls he had met in his first class this morning. She seemed quieter, more reserved, and he liked the thoughtful way she answered him. She was exactly the kind of person he had been hoping to meet.

Suddenly something occurred to him. "Elizabeth Wakefield," he said, "would it be possible for us to walk home together this afternoon after school?"

"Where are you staying, Arthur?" she asked.

"With the Richardsons. On Greenbriar Road."

"Greenbriar Road isn't too far from my house," Elizabeth replied with a smile. "I'll be happy to walk home with you, but please, just call me Elizabeth. I hope you won't mind if I ask you some questions while we walk," she added. "I'm very curious about your country, especially about the things that are happening there now. Our student newspaper is going to put out a special edition on current events in Santa Dora."

Arthur nodded. "I will be glad to answer your questions, Elizabeth," he said. He hesitated, remembering something that had been bothering him ever since this morning. "But I also have a question of my own."

"What is it?" Elizabeth asked.

He frowned. "Could you tell me, please," he said, "why a girl would call herself a Unicorn?"

Elizabeth's eyes twinkled. "That's a long story," she said with a laugh. "Maybe we'd better save it for our walk home."

Arthur nodded happily. "Until this afternoon," he agreed.

Three

◇

Leaving school with Arthur that afternoon, Elizabeth discovered, was quite an experience. Everybody wanted to ask him questions about Santa Dora.

Caroline Pearce was first. She stopped Arthur by the drinking fountain. "Excuse me, Arthur, but I'm doing a report on Santa Doran art. Who do you think is the most famous Santa Doran artist?"

"Jacques Marin, of course," Arthur answered without hesitation. "He painted some very beautiful pictures of the sea and fishing boats. Fishing is very important in our country. Lots of people make their living that way."

Caroline leaned forward. "Oh?" she asked, with great interest, "is that what *your* father does?"

Arthur shook his head. "No," he said, "it isn't."

Caroline waited a moment, but when Arthur didn't offer any more information, she thanked him and left.

A little further on, Charlie Cashman and Jerry McAllister were waiting by the door. "Hey, Art, we're doing a model of the Chateau Royale," Jerry told him. "You know, the old fort?"

Arthur nodded happily. He seemed to enjoy being called by his nickname. "Yes," he said, "everybody in Santa Dora knows the Chateau Royale. It is the oldest building in our country." He grinned. "Once upon a time, back in the fourteenth century, it was a prison."

"What we want to know," Charlie said, "is whether they still use those old guns."

"Yeah," Jerry chimed in, "the king lives there, doesn't he? Does he let the guards fire the guns sometimes?"

Elizabeth saw that Arthur was beginning to look a little uneasy. She wasn't surprised. If she were an exchange student and strangers kept popping up with weird questions about America, she'd be uncomfortable, too. What if she couldn't answer them all?

But Arthur had an answer to this one. "Yes," he said slowly, "the royal family lives there." He smiled a little. "And yes, the guns are used, but only on state occasions. The Santa Doran palace guards fire a salute and the royal family greets the people from a balcony of the Chateau."

"Wow," Jerry exclaimed. "Would I love to see that!"

"So, how does it feel to be such a celebrity?" Elizabeth asked him once they had escaped the crowded school grounds.

"A celebrity?" Arthur asked, his dark eyes widening. He was startled by the question, even a little edgy.

"Well, you're the very first Sweet Valley Middle School exchange student," she explained. "And you've certainly been the center of attention today, starting with this morning. Just walking out of school with you was like walking with a movie star."

Arthur nodded, regaining his composure. "I understand," he said. "Yes, indeed, everyone is very nice and very friendly. And I enjoy answering questions about my country. It is truly a pleasure to me that Americans are interested in Santa Dora. But . . ." He hesitated.

"But what?" Elizabeth prodded gently.

"But *I* am interested in America!" Arthur burst out, sounding frustrated. "I had hoped to learn a great deal about *your* country while I was here.

And in all this study of Santa Dora at school," he added mournfully, "there is no time for me to learn about America!"

Elizabeth couldn't help remembering what she had said to Jessica the night before. What Arthur needed was for somebody to show him the way they lived, what they did for fun, and how they enjoyed themselves. "Yes," she said, nodding, "I can certainly understand that."

"I do not wish to appear ungrateful," Arthur said.

"You're not," Elizabeth assured him. "Not at all. If I were visiting Santa Dora, I wouldn't want to be talking about California *all* the time."

"Exactly." Arthur smiled. "Everyone is making a special effort to make me feel at home, but what I really want is to feel like I am in America!"

"I'll talk to some of my friends," Elizabeth said thoughtfully, "and see what we can come up with." She glanced at him and smiled. "Are you ready to hear about the Unicorns now?"

"I'm glad you remembered," Arthur said. He shook his head, looking puzzled. "All day this affair of the Unicorn has been a great mystery to me."

Elizabeth nodded. "It's a club—a group of girls who do things together. They chose the name because Unicorns are very beautiful and special creatures, and they believe that they are equally as beautiful and special."

"Oh." Arthur raised one eyebrow. "What do these Unicorns do?"

"They hold meetings and . . ." Elizabeth tried to think of other activities to tell Arthur about, but she drew a blank. Mostly they talked about clothes and boys—and girls who aren't Unicorns. But she didn't want to tell Arthur that. "They usually wear something purple," she added, finishing her sentence.

"The color of royalty, right?" Arthur mused.

Elizabeth smiled. "Yes. That's why they chose it."

"I see." Arthur studied her. "You are not a Unicorn, Elizabeth?"

Elizabeth shook her head with a little laugh. "No. My twin sister, Jessica, is, though. That's why I know so much about them."

"But you are beautiful. And special."

Elizabeth blushed at his compliment. "Thank you," she said. After a moment, she added, "Jessica and the Unicorns are very interested in Santa Dora's royal family. They'll probably be asking you plenty of questions."

Arthur hesitated. "I see," he said. "I'll try my

best to answer them." But from the sound of his voice, Elizabeth got the feeling that he wasn't looking forward to their questions.

After saying goodbye to Arthur, Elizabeth hurried to Amy's house, where Amy, Julie Porter, and Sophia Rizzo were planning the special edition of *The Sweet Valley Sixers*. While she was walking, a different idea came to her, and by the time she got to Amy's house, she was breathless with excitement.

"Hi, Elizabeth," Amy greeted her. "What did you find out from Arthur? Are there any current events that he thinks we ought to feature in the newspaper?"

"I didn't ask him," Elizabeth confessed. "Actually, we got to talking about what *he* wanted to learn while he was here. And that gave me an idea."

"A *new* idea?" Sophia asked. She looked around at the clippings scattered on the floor where they were sitting. "But we've already gotten started on *this* one."

"We can do both," Elizabeth said confidently. She sat down on the floor beside Sophia and crossed her legs.

The girls all looked at her attentively. "What do you have in mind, Elizabeth?" Amy asked.

"Arthur says he's glad that everybody's trying to make him feel at home by asking questions about Santa Dora," Elizabeth told them. "But what he would really like is to feel he's in America."

"We can handle that easily," Amy interrupted, tugging on a strand of her blond hair. "We can take him to the mall. There's nothing more American than going shopping. We can show him the sporting goods store and the hobby shop."

"And there's the pet shop," Sophia added, her brown eyes shining. "And the bookstore."

"And the record store," Julie added. Julie loved music. "We could do it tomorrow, after school."

"Great!" Elizabeth smiled happily at her friends. She could always count on them to come up with fabulous ideas. Arthur had given her his phone number—in a minute she would call him and ask if he'd go with them after school.

Amy was watching her, head tilted to one side. "But those are *our* ideas," she reminded Elizabeth. "You haven't told us *yours* yet."

Elizabeth nodded. "Well, I still think the special edition is a good idea, but it's all about Santa Dora. It'll be easy to do, since we've already gotten such a good collection of clippings and we can just run them off on the copy machine. But now I think we ought to do something else, too. Something that Arthur can take home with him."

"Like what?" Julie asked curiously.

"Like a scrapbook," Elizabeth said. "A scrapbook about America, put together by the whole sixth grade. It will remind him about what America is really like."

"But what could we put in a scrapbook?" Sophia asked, wrinkling her forehead.

"What about some of my best baseball cards?" Amy offered excitedly. "I'll bet he'd love the ones with the California Angels on them."

Julie nodded. "And I could put in the program I got when Mom and Dad took me to the All-America Music Festival last summer. In fact," she added thoughtfully, "maybe we could do a couple of pages on music. We could include some TV and movie stuff, too."

"I've got some campaign buttons from the last presidential election," Elizabeth added. "We could do a couple of pages on American politics."

"And how about some recipes for a Fourth of July picnic?" Sophia asked. "There's nothing more American than the Fourth!" She clapped her hands. "Oh, I'm so glad you thought of this, Elizabeth! Arthur will love it!"

"Yes," Amy exclaimed, "and the best part is that he can take it all home with him!" She jumped up. "I'll go look for those baseball cards right now."

"And I've got a scrapbook we can use," Julie said happily.

"Great," Elizabeth said. Her smile got broader. "Hey, maybe we could even have a page of American slang!"

At home, Jessica had just invented a new kind of sandwich—avocado-and-banana—for herself. She loved to snack, but this afternoon she wasn't in a very good mood. She, Lila and Ellen had been waiting to talk to Arthur after school, but Elizabeth had snatched him out from under their very noses.

Of course, she reflected, as she spread mayonnaise on her bread, Arthur was free to do whatever he wanted. But the Unicorns needed some information about Santa Doran food for their party and Jessica had questions for her report. It just wasn't fair for Elizabeth to drag him off all by herself.

"Well, I'm glad to see that you're finally home," Jessica snapped, as Elizabeth came into the Wake-

field kitchen and put her books on the table.
"I hope you got enough of Arthur for one
day!"

Elizabeth stared at her sister. "I walked home
with him, if that's what you mean," she said quietly. She went to the refrigerator and opened it.
"He asked me to."

"But Lila, Ellen and I wanted to find out some
stuff for the party," Jessica pouted. She sat down
and took a big bite out of her sandwich. "And
after all the work we did on the welcome this
morning, it really wasn't fair for you to run off
with him."

"I'm sorry, Jess," Elizabeth said, pouring a glass
of milk for herself and one for her sister. "But
you'll have plenty of time to talk to him tomorrow. And I'm sure he'll be eager to talk to you. He
was curious about the Unicorns."

"Oh, really?" Jessica sipped her milk, softening
a little. "Well, then, I'll catch him first thing in the
morning. And maybe it would be a good time to
invite him to eat lunch with the Unicorns tomorrow. We still have some of our Santa Doran pastries left over—I'm sure he'd enjoy having one for
dessert. They'll remind him of home."

Elizabeth rolled her eyes.

"Oh, Lizzie," Jessica went on. "Isn't he *cute*,

with that dark curly hair and his gorgeous dark eyes? And isn't his accent absolutely *adorable*?''

"Yes, he is cute," Elizabeth said thoughtfully. "And he's nice, too. But don't you think that he might like an American dessert? A big piece of apple pie with ice cream, maybe, or some angel food cake?''

"But those are so *ordinary*," Jessica objected, dismissing Elizabeth's suggestion with a shake of her head.

"Maybe he'd *rather* experience some everyday American things," Elizabeth said. She sat down across the table from Jessica and leaned forward eagerly. "Let me tell you about the scrapbook Amy, Julie, Sophia and I are planning, Jess. We're going to ask everybody to contribute something really *American* for Arthur to take home with him. It doesn't have to be expensive or fancy. It should just represent something very American."

Jessica frowned. "What kind of stuff, Elizabeth?"

"Well, Amy's going to contribute some baseball cards, and Sophia's putting in recipes for a Fourth of July picnic and—"

"Recipes?" Jessica interrupted with a giggle. "Baseball cards? Oh, come on, Lizzie, be serious!" She took another bite out of her sandwich, shaking her head. "Do you really think someone from such an exciting place will be interested in those things? You get the weirdest ideas sometimes."

"I think he'll like them. Do you have anything I could include, Jess?"

"Well, I've got a picture of Johnny Buck you can have. It's not autographed or anything, but maybe Arthur would like it. And a little red, white, and blue flag sticker."

"That's perfect, Jess. We'll put the flag sticker on the very front page."

"OK. If you really want them." Jessica gave Elizabeth a pitying look. Sometimes she couldn't believe they were twins.

Four

◇

"Just look." Amy nudged Elizabeth and pointed at Arthur, who was walking through the toy store, engrossed in the items on the shelves. "Doesn't he look like he's having a great time?"

Elizabeth had to agree. For the last hour, the four of them—Elizabeth, Amy, Julie, and Sophia— had been following Arthur around the Sweet Valley Mall, trying to answer the hundreds of questions he was throwing at them. He seemed to have lost much of his shyness and reserve, and Elizabeth was delighted that he was laughing and joking with them.

Arthur turned around. "What's that?" he demanded, pointing to a round plastic disc hanging on the wall.

"It's a Frisbee," Amy explained.

"A Frisbee?" Arthur repeated, mystified.

"Sure," Amy said. "You throw it. Like this." She slung an imaginary Frisbee across the room. Elizabeth giggled. It was a good try, but without seeing a Frisbee in action, it was probably pretty hard to follow what Amy was doing.

Arthur frowned. "I don't understand," he said. "Can you show me?"

"Sure," Amy replied. "But not in here."

"OK," Arthur said, "I'll buy it and we can take it to the parking lot."

Elizabeth laughed. "Don't you think you've got enough?" she asked, pointing to the two shopping bags full of things Arthur had already bought. There was a football, a baseball bat, a stuffed Texas longhorn steer, a pair of Indian moccasins, a jackknife, a Johnny Buck album, a Confederate Army cap, and two pairs of jeans. In the other bag there were books, mostly American classics: *The Wizard of Oz*, *Little House on the Prairie*, *The Adventures of Huckleberry Finn*, and an illustrated history of the Texas Rangers. He'd even bought a videotape of Walt Disney's *Alice in Wonderland*.

Arthur shook his head, looking serious. "But I'm learning so much about America!" he said. "Much more than I could ever learn at school."

"Right," Julie put in, "what teacher would ever demonstrate a Frisbee?"

Everybody laughed and then Arthur went off to pay for his purchase. When he came back, they left the mall and went out to the parking lot, where Mr. Sutton was going to pick them up. Amy showed him how to toss the Frisbee. They sailed it back and forth a few times, and then Arthur's attention was caught by something else.

"Oh, look," he said delightedly, pointing to a couple of kids on skates. "Roller skates!" He turned to Elizabeth. "Do you skate?"

"Doesn't everybody?" Elizabeth asked, laughing. "It's the great American pastime—almost as big as Little League baseball."

"Well, then, will you teach me?"

"Sure," Elizabeth answered happily. "Any time you're ready."

"*Great*," Arthur said emphatically, as they all climbed into the Suttons' car.

When they got to Amy's house, she invited them in for milk and oatmeal cookies—"another great American tradition," she told Arthur as she filled a glass for him.

"We've been showing you all sorts of things about the way we live in America," Elizabeth said, as they sat around the table. "Why don't you tell us how *you* live, back in Santa Dora?"

"Yeah," Sophia chimed in, looking curious, "what do your parents do? What kind of house do you live in?"

"Do you have brothers and sisters?" Amy wanted to know. "What do you do for fun?"

"Do you have things like dishwashers and washing machines in Santa Dora?" Julie asked.

Elizabeth smiled at the barrage of questions. They couldn't help being curious about someone from another country. But Arthur was acting kind of shy again. He nibbled at his cookie, not looking at them. "I . . . uh, my father is in the government," he said hesitantly. "And my mother . . . well, she does lots of things."

"Like what?" Julie prompted.

Arthur stood up. "I think," he said, glancing at his watch, "that it is time for me to go. I promised Mrs. Richardson that I wouldn't be late for supper. Thank you so much for the milk and cookies," he said politely as he shook each girl's hand. "And for the Frisbee lesson." He smiled.

Amy frowned. "I'm sorry you have to go so soon," she said. "We were just getting warmed up. There's *so* much we want to know!"

"Perhaps another time," Arthur said, and left.

"Did you notice," Amy said to her friends when Arthur had gone, "that he didn't seem very anxious to answer our questions?"

Elizabeth nodded. She *had* noticed. And she was remembering the comments of several of the kids at school. Arthur couldn't seem to ask enough questions about the American way of life. But when it came to answering questions about himself and the way he lived back in Santa Dora, he usually changed the subject as fast as he could. Elizabeth wondered why.

At lunch the next day, Jessica and the Unicorns, with Brooke Dennis's help, had organized a Santa Doran sing-along. They passed out mimeographed sheets with the words to a half-dozen folk songs, and everybody sang. Arthur, sitting at the Unicorns' table, stood up and politely thanked the group when the singing was over. From a distance, Elizabeth thought he looked relieved.

After finishing his lunch, Arthur went over to the table where Elizabeth was eating with Amy. "I understand," he said, "that there is a beach nearby. Would you both like to go there with me after school today?"

"That's a great idea," Elizabeth said. "I'd love to go to the beach."

Amy sighed. "I'm afraid I can't make it," she said, wrinkling her nose. "I promised Mrs. Sampson I'd babysit this afternoon."

"Oh, that's too bad, Amy," Elizabeth said. "But I'd still like to go, Arthur. If you want to, we could ride bikes to the beach. You could borrow Jessica's." She glanced toward the Unicorn table, remembering her conversation with Jessica after school on Monday. "But I don't want to . . . well, to take up all of your time. I know there are other classmates who would like to show you some places, too."

Arthur smiled reassuringly. "But I want to go to the beach with *you*, Elizabeth."

That afternoon, Elizabeth and Arthur parked their bikes in the bike rack and walked down toward the ocean, barefoot. For a while they tossed Arthur's new Frisbee back and forth, and Elizabeth showed him some tricks he could play with it. Then they walked along the shoreline a short distance. Arthur was fascinated by the huge Pacific breakers that rose up a half-mile off the beach. And he couldn't keep his eyes off the surfers, whose bodies flashed like gleaming fish in and out of the enormous rollers.

"How wonderful," he kept saying. "It looks like such fun—I wish *I* could do that!"

"But I thought Santa Dora was on the seacoast," Elizabeth said. "Doesn't your family go to the beach on weekends?"

After a minute's hesitation, Arthur said, "Our beaches in Santa Dora are very crowded, because people come from all over Europe to lie in the sun. They are also not so sandy, and there's no surf." He gazed in disbelief as one of the surfers did a barrel roll and emerged right-side-up out of the frothing surf. He turned around and pointed to half-dozen boys on skateboards, doing wheelies and tilts along the sloping edge of the parking lot. "We don't have skateboarders, either. At least, not as many as you do."

Elizabeth nodded. "Surfing and skateboarding— the two great California sports." She looked at her watch. "It's getting late. We should probably head back. I have to be home in time to help with dinner tonight."

Arthur turned and smiled, his teeth flashing white. "Do we have time to get something to drink first?" he asked. "All this water is making me thirsty."

"Have you had a milk shake yet?" Elizabeth asked.

"A milk shake?" Arthur asked doubtfully. "No, I don't think that Mrs. Richardson shakes up the milk before she pours it."

Elizabeth laughed delightedly. "Then I know just the place," she said. "Come on!" They raced through the sand to their bikes and rode to the mall, where they went into Casey's and ordered two thick chocolate shakes. At the cash register, Arthur insisted on paying.

"You have been so kind to spend time with me," he said. "You can at least let me buy you a milk shake."

"Thank you," Elizabeth said, smiling. Arthur was so polite. Most American boys she knew would insist on going dutch.

Arthur pulled his wallet out of his pocket and reached for his bills. As he pulled out three American dollars and handed them to the clerk, a purple-and-white Santa Doran banknote fluttered onto the floor.

"I'll get it," Elizabeth said, bending over to pick it up.

Arthur gasped. "No, let me," he said, frantically reaching for the bill.

"That's OK," Elizabeth said. "I have it." She turned away from Arthur and held the bill up to the light. "I love to look at money from other countries," she said, studying the bill closely. "It's always prettier than ours. And it never seems quite real, somehow."

Then, suddenly, Elizabeth realized why Arthur hadn't wanted her to see the bill. The picture in the middle of the note looked exactly like Arthur. In fact, it *was* Arthur!

Five

◇

Elizabeth stared at the bill. "Arthur!" she gasped. "This is *you*!"

Arthur heaved a big sigh. "So now you know," he said wearily. He pocketed the change the clerk gave him and handed Elizabeth her chocolate shake. "Come on. Let's sit down and talk."

Still stunned, Elizabeth followed Arthur to a seat in the corner. "I'm not sure I understand," she said breathlessly, as they sat down. "Who *are* you?"

Arthur gave her a long look. "My name," he said in a low voice, "is Arthur Castillo. I am the son of King Armand and Queen Stephanie of Santa Dora."

"*Prince* Arthur?" Elizabeth squeaked.

Arthur nodded. His face looked grim. "That's why I haven't talked much about the life I lead back home. I didn't want to lie, but I didn't want to have to admit who I am, either."

Elizabeth could hardly catch her breath. A real live prince—sitting across the table from her, sipping a chocolate shake just like an ordinary person! A prince in disguise! It was unbelievable, like something out of a fairy tale.

"But why didn't you *tell* us, Ar—?" She stopped, feeling suddenly awkward and stiff. She took her elbows off the table and sat up straight. "Excuse me," she said, "but how—what exactly am I supposed to call you? Your Highness?"

Arthur pushed his shake away, looking sad. "You see? That's exactly the problem. The minute you found out who I was, you started worrying about how you should act. Isn't that true?"

"Well, yes," she admitted, "I guess I did. But it's only natural. After all, you don't meet royalty every day." She flushed. "I mean, *I* don't meet royalty every day. I'm not sure how to behave."

"I know." Arthur sighed heavily. "Believe me, I know. And that's exactly why I haven't told people who I am. They forget all about being friends and start trying to remember their manners. And even worse, they dream up all kinds of things that they think a prince likes to do. A tour of the local museums, or an evening of Beethoven and Mozart at the local symphony." He rolled his eyes. "I've heard Beethoven's Fifth Symphony so many times, I think I could conduct it in my sleep!"

Elizabeth couldn't help giggling a little. She hadn't even thought of it before, but of course the life of a prince must have its difficult sides. It would be awfully hard to be on public display *all* the time.

Arthur leaned forward, looking earnestly into her eyes. "Elizabeth, I've dreamed my whole life about seeing how other children live. But that can never happen back home, because everybody knows that I'm the heir to the throne. They all treat me like a celebrity."

Elizabeth squirmed, remembering how upset Arthur had been when she had called him a celebrity.

"Here, nobody knows who I am," Arthur continued. "As far as they're concerned, I'm just a regular boy, visiting another country for the first time. And I want it to stay that way. No museum tours, no Beethoven." His voice was very urgent.

"Please, Elizabeth, will you help me keep my secret?"

"Of course," Elizabeth promised warmly. "Of course I will, Arthur."

"It's going to be hard," Arthur warned her. "It will be a big temptation to tell your friends. You'll just have to forget we've had this conversation."

"But I understand how important this is to you, Arthur," Elizabeth said. "And I won't tell a soul. I promise."

"Thank you, Elizabeth," Arthur said. His dark eyes were grateful. "I know I can trust you."

The next morning, Arthur got out of bed with a firm determination. He had worried all night about all the kids at Sweet Valley Middle School finding out who he was. He had to talk to Elizabeth this morning before homeroom, and tell her once more how important it was that she not tell a soul about his real identity.

As he was walking out the door for school, the phone rang. It was his mother, calling from Los Angeles, full of news about the royal visit and questions about Arthur's stay in Sweet Valley. By the time he got to school, homeroom was already over.

Then when he got to science class, Elizabeth wasn't there. His heart sank and he couldn't help worrying.

Finally, between second and third periods, he spotted her in the hallway.

"Elizabeth," he called anxiously, hurrying to catch up with her, "I'm so glad to see you."

"But I—" she began.

"Listen, Elizabeth," Arthur said, putting his hand on her arm. "About what I told you yesterday. The secret, I mean."

Her blue-green eyes widened a little, and she nodded.

"I just want to make sure," Arthur went on, not giving her a chance to speak, "that you under-stand how important it is not to let anybody know about my family." He grinned a little. "Believe me, once people find out you're a prince, they never act the same."

She took a deep breath, then nodded again. "I understand," she said, in a low voice.

"Thanks," Arthur said, bowing a little. "I knew you would." He turned and went on his way, whistling happily to himself, sure that his secret was safe with Elizabeth.

Jessica stared after Arthur as he turned and went

down the hall. His words were still ringing in her ears. "Once people find out that you're a prince . . ." A *prince*! Excitement tumbled through her like a huge wave, and she could feel the goosebumps popping out all over her arms. Arthur Castle was really the boy she had read about—Arthur Castillo, Prince of Santa Dora— traveling incognito! And *she* was the only person who knew!

But then Jessica bit her lip. No, she wasn't the only person who knew. Obviously, Arthur had mistaken her for Elizabeth. She could see how serious Arthur was about not revealing his identity, but she couldn't imagine *why*. If she were a princess, she'd want the entire world to know about it! What possible reason could Arthur have for hiding who he was?

Jessica took a deep breath and walked down the crowded hallway, oblivious to the pushing and shoving around her. Obviously, Arthur wanted her, Elizabeth, to keep his secret. But how *could* she? The Unicorns would be absolutely *thrilled* if they knew Arthur was a member of the royal family. A real prince, right here at Sweet Valley Middle School! She imagined herself dancing with him at the Unicorns' party the following week. Now that their party was being given in honor of real, live royalty, it would be even *more* fabulous. And dancing with Prince Arthur would be almost as wonderful as being a princess herself.

Jessica narrowed her blue-green eyes. *She* hadn't promised Arthur not to tell who he was. It was Elizabeth who had done that. And anyway, this was the sort of secret that just begged to be shared. And think of the points she would score with Janet Howell, the president of the Unicorns, when she revealed Arthur's real identity! Jessica made up her mind. She would call an emergency meeting of the Unicorns that afternoon, right after school. She really had no choice.

Janet Howell rapped for order on the coffee table in Lila's den. "As everyone knows, Jessica has mysteriously called this special meeting of the Unicorns, and now I think it's time for her to tell us what it's all about."

"Yes," Lila echoed. "I had to cancel my haircut appointment just for this. It'd better be good."

"Well, you won't be disappointed, Lila." Jessica paused for dramatic effect, and looked around at the group. "I have a very important announcement to make."

She paused again. Janet sighed loudly and Lila rolled her eyes.

"As you all know, Arthur Castle is visiting us from Santa Dora," Jessica began.

Ellen Riteman spoke up impatiently. "Jessica," she said, "I thought you were going to tell us something *new*. Of course we all know about Arthur. We're giving him a fabulous party, remember?"

"Please, Ellen, give me a chance to finish. Arthur Castle," Jessica went on, "isn't *really* Arthur Castle." She leaned forward and lowered her voice to a whisper. "His real name is Arthur *Castillo* and he is a prince of the Santa Doran royal family."

Mary Wallace gasped loudly but none of the other Unicorns even reacted.

Janet Howell frowned. "Where did you find this out, Jessica?" she asked. "It sure sounds made up to me. The next thing you know, you'll be telling us that you're the long-lost princess of Santa Dora!"

As usual, Lila took her cue from Janet. "Yeah, Jessica. Sounds like you got the wrong information."

Jessica lifted her chin and gave Lila a lofty glance. "I did not, Lila. I found this out from Prince Arthur himself," she said proudly. "He told me this morning."

Janet laughed scornfully. "And you *fell* for it? Really, Jessica!" She shook her head, a snobbish look on her face. "Arthur Castle is an ordinary exchange student. He's no prince."

Jessica went on as if Janet hadn't said anything. "After he told me, I decided to double check something in a book I had used for my oral report. I went to the library and looked through tons of books on Santa Dora. And I finally found it."

"What?" Lila asked, showing some interest.

"*This*," Jessica said with a triumphant smile. She laid the book, open, on the coffee table, and pointed to a small picture at the bottom of one page. It was a photograph of King Armand, Queen Stephanie and their son, the crown prince of Santa Dora, all wearing their royal crowns and robes. "See," she said smugly. "If you look closely, you'll see that *Arthur* is the crown prince!"

All the girls leaned forward and examined the tiny photograph. Mary was the first to speak. "Jessica's right!" she exclaimed. "It *is* Arthur! You have to look real close, but it's him!"

Lila and Janet nodded, too.

"And Ar—, uh, *Prince* Arthur told you this himself?" Janet asked.

Jessica nodded. It wasn't necessary to tell them that Prince Arthur had mistaken her for her sister.

"Yes," she said. "He's kept it a secret because . . ." She hesitated. She still didn't understand *why* Arthur wouldn't tell anybody. "Because his parents wanted him to . . . for security reasons," she finished. "After all, if you're the prince, you probably have to be pretty careful of the places you go and the people you talk to."

"I'm sorry I didn't believe you at first, Jessica," Janet said.

There was a general murmur of agreement around the table.

"Oh, that's OK," Jessica said, picking up her library book. "I don't blame you. It *is* hard to believe."

"Well, now that we know," Janet said importantly, resuming command, "we have to decide what we should *do* about it."

"I think that we ought to adjourn until tomorrow," Lila said. "We've already scheduled a meeting to work on decorations for the party. Let's talk about this more then."

"I think that's a good idea," Janet said. "This meeting is now adjourned."

That night after dinner, Elizabeth began to clear off the dinner table.

"Where did Jessica go?" Mrs. Wakefield asked, picking up the butter dish and empty salad bowl.

Elizabeth grinned. "She went to the library," she said.

Steven Wakefield, the twins' older brother, grabbed the last roll off the plate as he got up from the table. "The library?" he asked, raising his eyes toward the ceiling in mock surprise. "You mean Jessica is actually going to *study*? I don't believe it."

Mrs. Wakefield paused in the doorway. "It does seem a little odd, doesn't it?"

"She's working on a Unicorn project," Elizabeth told them. "They're getting ready for a party next week."

"How can she work on a party at the library?" Steven muttered. He crammed the roll into his mouth and headed for the garage. "This is really weird."

The doorbell rang. "I'll get it," Elizabeth said, putting her dishes down.

She opened the door to find Arthur. A pair of roller skates hung by the laces over his shoulder. "Hi, Elizabeth," he said. "I thought I'd stop by to see if you wanted to give me a skating lesson tonight."

"Sure, Arthur. That would be great. I just have to finish doing the dishes."

"I'll help," Arthur offered promptly.

Giggling at the idea of a prince doing the dishes, Elizabeth led the way to the kitchen, where she introduced Arthur to her mother. They began to load the dishwasher.

While they worked, Arthur told Elizabeth about his day at school and Elizabeth explained that she hadn't been in science class because of a dentist appointment. When they were finished in the kitchen, they went out to the Wakefields' front yard and laced up their skates.

"I'm not sure I'll be very good at this," Arthur said apprehensively. He stood up, wobbling a little. "I went ice skating in Switzerland once, but I've never been on roller skates before."

"Well, if you ice skate you probably have a good sense of balance," Elizabeth told him. "Come on— you'll get the hang of it. In a few minutes, you'll be skating like a pro!"

" 'The hang of it?' " Arthur asked doubtfully.

"You'll get used to it," Elizabeth translated. "Come on."

After a few false starts, Arthur was roller-skating like a native Californian. He and Elizabeth spent the next hour skating around the neighborhood, laughing and having fun.

When it was time to go home, Arthur gave Elizabeth a big smile. "When I'm with you, Liz," he said, "I can almost forget—"

"Sshh!" Elizabeth reminded him, grinning. "There isn't anything to forget. We're just two regular kids, that's all. We did the dishes, and we've been having a great time roller-skating."

Arthur laughed. "You know, I've been thinking," he said. "About the party the Unicorns are giving. Would you go with me, Elizabeth?"

Elizabeth smiled. "Yes," she agreed with pleasure, "I'll be glad to go with you, Arthur."

Six

◇

"I still can't believe it," Ellen Riteman said. "A *prince*! Right here in Sweet Valley! It's almost too good to be true."

"Actually," Janet Howell put in, "there's no doubt that it *is* true. I saw on the TV news last night that the king and queen of Santa Dora were guests at some big society gala in Los Angeles. Of course," she added, "the news didn't say anything about the prince, but I guess Jessica's right. They're probably keeping it a secret for security reasons."

"But that's silly," Lila said. "Nobody here in Sweet Valley would want to hurt the prince."

Smiling a little, Jessica flipped through Elizabeth's history book about Santa Dora. Now that they were planning a party for *royalty*, it was absolutely crucial that every detail be correct so she was really studying the book closely.

"Did you get the picture of the Chateau Royale courtyard from Charlie?" she asked Ellen. Ellen nodded. "With a little work, we can make the patio look exactly like it. And with all the entertainment, Arthur will think he's back at home, in the middle of a Santa Doran festival." She paused thoughtfully. "But don't we need someplace special for the prince to sit and watch the festival?"

"I know what we need," Lila exclaimed. "We need a *throne!*"

"Oh, you're right, Lila!" Ellen agreed, nodding. "With a canopy overhead."

"A throne with a canopy would look terrific," Jessica said. "I'll bet Arthur—*Prince* Arthur will be terribly impressed. Maybe he'll even make the Unicorns honorary royalty or something."

"You know what we *really* need," Lila said, wrinkling her forehead. "We need to know how to behave around a prince. We certainly don't want to offend him or embarrass ourselves."

Jessica nodded eagerly. "I've been thinking about the same thing," she said. "That's why I went to the library again last night." She reached down into her purse and pulled out a slender book. "This book is called *Etiquette for Special Occasions*, and it covers things like how to address a king and how to curtsy and stuff like that."

"Jessica," Mary said with a smile, "you think of *everything*!"

"Does it tell how to talk to a prince?" Ellen asked.

"It says that you should call him 'Your Royal Highness,'" Jessica reported, flipping through the pages. "But you're not supposed to look *at* him. You're supposed to look down. And you're supposed to murmur it respectfully, not talk loudly or yell. And of course, a prince doesn't open doors for himself or pull out chairs or anything like that. Other people are supposed to do that for him. They should make sure that all he has to do is walk and sit and bow once in a while."

Mary was looking amused. "What about curtsying?" she asked. "I don't think I can manage a curtsy, Jessica. I'll fall on my face."

"You can do it, Mary," Jessica assured her. "It just takes a little practice, that's all." And she got up and executed a graceful-looking curtsy, bending her knees just right and holding the hem of her long T-shirt the way she would a dress. She'd spent a few minutes practicing in front of her bedroom mirror the night before. She didn't want to look awkward the first time she curtsied to Prince Arthur.

"Do it again, Jessica," Ellen said.

"Yes," Janet put in bossily. "I think we *all* ought to practice. After all, when we see Prince Arthur at school on Monday, we don't want to treat him like an ordinary person! That would be a terrible insult!"

"I'll be glad to teach you," Jessica offered graciously. So for the next half hour, under Jessica's direction, the Unicorns practiced curtsying to one another and murmuring, "Yes, Your Royal Highness," and "No, Your Royal Highness," and "So kind of you to say so, Your Royal Highness."

"Aren't you dressed yet, Jessica?" Elizabeth asked, coming into her twin's room on Saturday night. "Mom and Dad are almost ready to go to the movie." She glanced around. As usual, Jessica's pretty pink-and-white room was in chaos, with clothes lying around everywhere and magazines and records piled in messy stacks on the floor.

"In a minute," Jessica replied in a muffled voice. She emerged from the closet with a dress in her hand. "I'm trying to find something to wear to the Unicorns' party on Thursday night."

Elizabeth laughed. "But this is only *Saturday*,"

she pointed out. "Don't you think you're rushing it just a little?"

"But the party is so important!" Jessica exclaimed. "I have to look absolutely perfect!" She held up a pink-and-white ruffled dress with a full skirt and little puffed sleeves. "Do you think this will do, or should I buy something new?"

"That'll be fine. You'll look great." Elizabeth glanced curiously at her sister. "Why is this party so important?"

"Because Arthur—because it's in honor of Arthur," Jessica stammered. She half-turned away. "We've been working awfully hard on it, Liz. It's going to be a wonderful party, with lots of music and dancing. Lila's father's caterer is going to make some great Santa Doran food, and—"

"A *caterer*?" Elizabeth asked sharply. "Come on, Jessica, don't you think that's going a little too far? If you asked Arthur what he wanted, he'd probably pick hot dogs and ice cream, and he'd probably be a lot happier if we all put on shorts and went to a Little League game."

Jessica laughed. "Oh, Elizabeth, you're a riot. A Little League game? For a—for an exchange student? Don't be silly." She glanced at her sister. "You *are* coming to the party, aren't you?"

Elizabeth nodded. "As a matter of fact," she said happily, "I'm going with—"

But she didn't get to finish her sentence. "Girls!" Mr. Wakefield called from downstairs, "your mother and I are ready to go. Come on, or we'll miss the start of the movie!"

"Coming, Dad," Elizabeth called. With Jessica right behind her, she hurried downstairs.

On Sunday afternoon, Elizabeth and the other *Sixers* staffers were at Amy's house, finishing up the special edition of the newspaper and getting started on the scrapbook.

"It looks like we've already got a bunch of good stuff for Arthur," Julie said happily. She knelt down beside the box that contained all the memorabilia. "Oh, look. Somebody gave us a little Confederate flag."

"Yes," Elizabeth said, "that's from Jimmy Underwood. I told him that Arthur had already bought a Confederate cap." She reached into the box and pulled out a *TV Guide*. "And this is from Brooke Dennis. It's really special."

"A *TV Guide*?" Sophia echoed. "What's so special about that?"

"It's been autographed by Kent Kellerman," Elizabeth grinned. Kent was one of the biggest soap opera stars on TV.

"Kent Kellerman!" Amy squealed, reaching for it. "Let me see that!"

"Here's a postcard of Old Faithful," Julie said. "And a Denver Broncos pennant. And a pizza coupon that says 'We deliver anywhere.' "

Elizabeth laughed. "Arthur should get a kick out of that one. Imagine a pizza truck trying to get from Sweet Valley to Santa Dora." She held up something else. "Look—it's a Twinkies wrapper! And Randy Mason gave us a bunch of good American history stamps from his collection. We can have a whole page of stamps, if we want."

For an hour, the girls worked on the scrapbook, attaching items to the pages while they talked about the Unicorns' party coming up on Thursday, the evening before Arthur's last day at school.

"It really seems silly," Amy said. "All that big deal they're making about food and decorations, I mean. I don't think Arthur's the kind of boy who cares about that sort of thing." She made a face. "Those Unicorns—they always want to show off. If you ask me, this party isn't for Arthur, it's for *them.*"

Elizabeth tilted her head to one side. Amy always said exactly what she thought, and Elizabeth couldn't help agreeing with her. But she also wanted to stick up for Jess. She hated having anybody criticize her twin. "Well," she said, "even so, it's up to the rest of us to make sure that Arthur has a good time doing whatever it is he wants to do."

And that was exactly what she intended to do.

Seven

◇

As soon as she got to homeroom on Monday morning, Elizabeth looked for Arthur. She knew that he had spent the weekend at Disneyland with his parents, and she wanted to hear all about his trip. But Arthur was surrounded by Unicorns, all giggling and talking excitedly, and she couldn't get close to him.

"Boy, the Unicorns sure are acting weird," Amy said, coming up to her, "even for Unicorns." She pointed. "Look at them. They're like a bunch of bees buzzing around a jar of honey."

Elizabeth shook her head as Ellen Riteman pulled out Arthur's chair for him. "You're right," she said, frowning. "I thought the newness of Arthur's visit was beginning to wear off a little. But they're acting even more excited than they did the day he came!"

Her frown deepened when she saw that somebody had put a little bunch of flowers on Arthur's desk, tied with a purple ribbon. Obviously, the Unicorns were going all out to make sure that he noticed them.

Elizabeth felt worse when she spotted Jessica standing beside Arthur, offering him two cookies wrapped in a paper napkin and tied with *another* purple ribbon. And when he took them, she actually dropped a *curtsy*! This whole thing was getting really silly. Elizabeth just hoped Arthur could manage to keep his sense of humor.

What's going on? Arthur wondered. For the first time in his life, he'd been able to enjoy being a regular kid—shopping in the mall, riding bikes to the beach, going roller-skating. It had been terrific, and he was really grateful to Elizabeth for her friendship. She'd been the one who'd made it possible for him to feel so *ordinary*.

But now it was back to being the center of attention again—and even worse than last week! As the morning went on, Arthur noticed it more and more. In fact, the other students were treating him with such exaggerated respect that he was beginning to suspect that they'd found out who he was.

But the minute that thought occurred to Arthur, he pushed it away. They *couldn't* have found out—it wasn't possible. The only person who knew his identity was Elizabeth Wakefield, and he was certain that she wouldn't betray him.

Still, Arthur couldn't help suspecting that something was wrong, *terribly* wrong and he was determined to find out what it was by the end of the day.

At lunch hour, when Arthur entered the cafeteria, Janet Howell, an eighth grader who hadn't paid him any attention at all the week before, showed him to an empty table with a bouquet of purple irises on it. Then she curtsied deeply and murmured, "Here you are, Your Highness. We thought you might like to have some privacy while you ate your lunch."

Arthur stared at Janet. "Excuse me, but what did you call me?" he asked. Around him, the kids at the other tables had fallen silent, watching.

Janet looked flustered. "Did I—did I say it wrong?" she stammered hastily, her cheeks flushing red. "I mean, people are supposed to call you 'Your Highness,' aren't they?"

"So you know," Arthur said dully, as he sat

down in the chair Jessica Wakefield pulled out for him. At his *private* table.

"Yes, we know," Lila said, "and we can't tell you how *proud* we are that we have a member of the Santa Doran royal family here with us!"

"Thank you," Arthur said, automatically straightening his shoulders, "I am glad to be here." He lowered his glance to his tray and stared at his food. He had suddenly lost his appetite.

"Is there anything else we can get for you, Your Highness?" Jessica asked, hovering at his elbow.

"No, thank you," Arthur sighed. At the tables around him, the other kids went back to their lunches, with a subdued clatter. Arthur choked down a bite of his sandwich, feeling despondent. He didn't want to believe it, but there was only one explanation for what was happening. Elizabeth must have broken his confidence. Anger welled up inside him, but the hurt and disappointment was more bitter than the anger. It had happened before. Everytime he thought he'd made a true friend, he'd discover that the person was only interested in him because he was a prince. Elizabeth Wakefield was no different than the others.

Still, Elizabeth had seemed different, like the type of girl who would be more interested in you for who you *were*, than for what title you'd inherited from your family. Maybe it hurt even worse this time because he'd been fooled so completely. Because he'd really thought that Elizabeth was sincere.

He finished his lunch and the girls stepped forward again. "Would you like some ice cream, Your Highness?" Jessica asked, picking up his tray. "We have vanilla or chocolate."

"No, thank you," Arthur said politely. He managed a smile. "I guess I'm just not very hungry." No matter how upset he was at Elizabeth, he reminded himself, he still had to behave like a prince and bring credit to his country.

Arthur straightened his shoulders and pasted a small smile on his face. Then he walked across the cafeteria, while the students watched him in respectful silence. Well, he couldn't blame them. As far as they were concerned, princes weren't *real* people. A prince was somebody you read about in fairy tales, or saw in the movies. Somebody you had to be polite to, maybe even somebody you were a little afraid of.

But not somebody who would be a friend.

Elizabeth was just starting her homework when the phone rang. She ran to pick it up and was delighted to hear Arthur's voice. He'd been so mobbed by everybody this morning that she hadn't had a chance to talk to him. Then, just before lunch, *The Sixers* staff had gone on a brief field trip to the local newspaper with their English teacher and *The Sixers'* faculty supervisor, Mr. Bowman. They hadn't gotten back until after the last bell had rung.

"Hi, Arthur!" she exclaimed. "I've been wanting to talk to you all day. How was Disneyland? Did you have a good time?"

Arthur's voice was very quiet. "Elizabeth," he said, "everybody knows."

"Knows?" Elizabeth asked blankly. "Knows what?"

"Knows who I am." He paused and then burst out angrily, "You promised not to tell, Elizabeth. How could you do this to me? I thought we were friends!"

Elizabeth gasped. "What are you talking about, Arthur? I didn't tell anybody about you."

"Then how do they know? You are the only one I told."

"Are you *sure* they know?" Elizabeth frowned. Maybe it was Arthur's imagination.

"Of course I'm sure," Arthur said scornfully. "Somebody named Janet Howell called me 'Your

Highness.' And everybody's going around doing things for me. Things they think they ought to do for a prince." He sighed in resignation. "Don't try to convince me you didn't tell, Elizabeth. You're the *only* one who could have."

"Oh, Arthur," Elizabeth cried, almost in tears, "how can I convince you that I didn't have anything to do with it?"

"You can't," Arthur said flatly. "It's happened this way before. I think I've found a friend I can trust, and then I discover that the person isn't really a friend at all." His voice sounded sad and heavy. "But it's worse this time, Elizabeth. I trusted you, and you've ruined the only chance I've ever had to be just a normal boy."

"Arthur, it's not true!" Elizabeth wailed.

But all she heard was the click of the receiver in her ear.

Eight

◇

"Have you heard?" Jessica exclaimed excitedly, bursting into Elizabeth's bedroom twenty minutes later. "It was all over school today. Arthur Castle is a *prince*!"

Elizabeth rubbed her eyes tiredly. Ever since Arthur had ended their conversation, she'd been lying on her bed, trying to think, trying to figure out how she could get Arthur out of this terrible mess. But all she could think about was the sound of his voice when he said, "You've ruined the only chance I've ever had to be just a normal kid."

"Yes, I heard," she said unhappily. She looked at Jessica, wondering if somehow her twin had found out about Arthur and told everybody. "How did *you* find out, Jessica?"

Jessica gave her a quick glance. "From the Unicorns," she said, dismissing Elizabeth's question with a little shrug. "Everybody's talking about it. It's the news of the century. A *real* prince, right here in Sweet Valley."

Elizabeth flopped over onto her stomach. Spreading the word about Arthur was certainly the kind of thing that Jessica might do. But there was no reason to suspect her more than anyone else.

She sighed and said in a muffled voice, so low and sad that Jessica could barely hear her. "Arthur thinks I'm the one who told."

Jessica sucked in her breath. "You?"

"I didn't," Elizabeth said, "but he doesn't believe me. He blames me for the whole thing. We were friends, but now he's really upset. I don't think he's ever going to speak to me again."

Jessica stared down at her twin. "Oh, Lizzie, I'm *so* sorry," she exclaimed repentently, sitting down beside her sister and putting a hand on her shoulder. "That's terrible!"

Jessica *was* sorry she hadn't been more thoughtful. She was just thinking about how grateful the Unicorns would be to her for letting them in on such a wonderful secret. She hadn't even considered the possibility that it would get all over school so fast. Still, she couldn't blame her friends for telling other people. It wasn't exactly the kind of secret you could keep quiet. Anyway, there was nothing she could do now. And even though she *did* feel guilty, there was no reason to make matters worse by telling Elizabeth how the word had gotten out.

"Don't you think Arthur will get over it?" she asked, trying to keep her guilt from showing in her voice. "I don't understand—why was he keeping his identity secret in the first place? It's a pretty dumb thing to do."

"I don't think he'll get over it." Elizabeth sighed. "He was keeping his identity secret because he wanted to be able to act like an ordinary kid while he was in Sweet Valley. He didn't *want* people treating him like a prince. He wanted to make friends."

"But that's ridiculous," Jessica asserted firmly. "He *is* a prince!"

Elizabeth smiled glumly. "I think," she said, "that sometimes he just gets tired of people making a big fuss over him."

Jessica shook her head. "How could *anybody* get tired of being treated like royalty?" she wondered. She smiled at Elizabeth. She couldn't change what had happened, but maybe she could help a little.

"Anyway," she added, "I'll look for Arthur at school tomorrow and tell him it's not your fault that everybody knows."

"Whatever good that'll do," Elizabeth said unhappily. "I have the feeling that Arthur's made up his mind."

At school on Tuesday, Arthur didn't say a word to Elizabeth. In homeroom, he avoided looking in her direction, and when she got to science class, she discovered that he was sitting at a different table. Jessica seemed to have appointed herself his chief lady-in-waiting for the day, rushing around to make sure that he had the best of everything. Lila and Ellen were there, too, and even Janet Howell, during lunch periods. Arthur went along with all their suggestions politely, his shoulders set straight and a princely half-smile on his face. He was charming and gracious to everyone—except Elizabeth, of course. He wouldn't talk to her anymore.

"Listen, Elizabeth," Amy said, coming up to her when they were playing volleyball at recess, "we've decided that a scrapbook is just too *ordinary* for a prince. What do you think we ought to do with all this stuff we've collected?"

"Wait a minute," Elizabeth objected. "All that stuff is for *Arthur*."

"But a *prince* doesn't want a plain old scrapbook," Amy said. "He's probably got tons of scrapbooks at home, filled with newspaper clippings about his royal appearances."

"And some of our stuff is kind of silly," Sophia added worriedly. "I mean, what would a prince do with those old Fourth of July recipes? Why, he probably goes to a royal banquet every day of the week. And they certainly don't eat fried chicken and corn on the cob."

Elizabeth shook her head. "That's exactly why we ought to give it to him," she insisted. "All that ordinary American stuff will be very *special* to him. I'm sure that he won't think it's silly." There was a lump in her throat. She missed Arthur. She'd enjoyed the things they had done the week before and wished they could keep on doing them.

But this week, after school, the Unicorns were planning all sorts of cultural events for Arthur— events they thought were fit for a prince. On Tuesday afternoon, they took him to the Sweet Valley Historical Museum. There, they were met by a photographer from the newspaper who followed them around, snapping pictures while Janet Howell and Lila Fowler gave speeches about events of local interest.

On Wednesday evening, the Unicorns all put on their best outfits and took Arthur downtown to the civic center, where the Sweet Valley Symphony Orchestra was playing an evening of Mozart and Beethoven. The photographers were there again to take pictures of a special reception for Arthur, hosted by Lila Fowler's father. When Elizabeth read the newspaper headlines on Thursday morning, she couldn't help smiling a little, remembering what he had said the week before about knowing the Fifth Symphony so well that he could conduct it himself.

Elizabeth continued to work on the scrapbook project even though she knew that Arthur no longer liked her. And anyway, regardless of how Arthur felt about her, Elizabeth still liked him. How could you help but like somebody who endured the Unicorns' cultural blitz with such patience and politeness? Somebody who thanked them seriously when they scurried around opening doors, bowing and scraping? And she couldn't forget the fun she and Arthur had had the week before, tossing Frisbees, walking on the beach and drinking chocolate shakes at Casey's. She wanted Arthur to remember *those* things most of all, and the scrapbook would help to remind him. No matter how he felt about her, she would still be his friend. The scrapbook was one way of showing him that her friendship would endure.

After science on Thursday Elizabeth even attempted a conversation with him. She stopped by his table as everybody was leaving the classroom.

"I saw your picture in the paper again this morning, Arthur," she said. "The one that was taken last night at the symphony, with Lila's father."

"Yes." he said. Somewhere, down deep in his brown eyes, there was a ghost of a twinkle. "The orchestra played The Fifth Symphony."

Elizabeth shook her head. "I just don't understand," she said in a low voice, "why you're doing all these things you don't *want* to do. The museum, the women's club tea, the symphony."

Arthur looked at her. The twinkle was gone. "I don't have any choice, Elizabeth," he said soberly. "You Americans think that being a prince is all fun and games and having people do things for you. But it isn't. It's a big responsibility. Being a prince means touring museums and making little speeches to clubs and listening to music you don't particularly enjoy. As a prince, I represent my country, and I must be polite and friendly to everybody, all the time. I have to act interested, even when I'm bored. If I don't, it reflects on my country and on the royal family."

Elizabeth's eyes filled with tears. "Oh, Arthur," she said, "I feel just *terrible* about what's happened." And what made it worse was knowing that Arthur thought the whole thing was *her* fault.

Nine

◆

The week wasn't going the way Jessica had planned. When she told the Unicorns about Arthur, she'd gotten just what she'd wanted—lots of attention. Even Janet Howell had said how wonderful it was that Jessica had managed to find out Arthur's real identity. And since she was the one who'd found the book on etiquette, they'd looked to her to teach them how to curtsy and how to talk to Arthur. For a little while, Jessica had felt almost as important as Arthur. It had been a wonderful feeling.

But almost immediately the Unicorns' attention had shifted to Arthur himself, and now that they'd gotten comfortable in their new roles as ladies-in-waiting, none of them bothered to ask Jessica's opinion about anything. They just expected her to show up at the events they planned and stand around with the other Unicorns. Worse than that was the fact that Jessica didn't like museums or classical music. The tour through the museum had nearly bored her out of her mind, and the Sweet Valley Symphony Orchestra had actually put her to sleep!

Worst of all, Jessica could see how bad Elizabeth was feeling about the whole thing. She and Arthur had struck up a close friendship, and now he wouldn't even speak to her. Once or twice, Jessica had tried to raise the subject with Arthur, in a roundabout way. But he wouldn't even talk *about* Elizabeth, much less talk *to* her. And she had to be careful about how much she said. Jessica didn't want him to figure out what had really happened. Then he might be mad at *her*, instead of at Elizabeth. She just wished that Arthur hadn't been so touchy about his identity. Who would have guessed that he'd take it so hard?

But there was one bright spot—a *very* bright spot. Arthur had picked Jessica to be his escort to the Unicorns' party on Thursday night. Unfortunately, he hadn't seemed especially enthusiastic when he'd asked her. Maybe it was because she looked like Elizabeth.

But she pushed those thoughts out of her mind as quickly as they occurred to her. *She* was going to the Unicorns' gala with Prince Arthur, and she was going to make the most of it! Already the other Unicorns were dying of envy. Lila had asked her what she was going to wear and Ellen had wanted to know if the etiquette book said anything about whether a girl could ask a prince to dance with her.

The night of the party, Elizabeth sat in her room, feeling miserable. Jessica and Arthur had already left for the party, and her parents had gone to a meeting. Elizabeth was all alone in the house.

Up until this afternoon, Elizabeth had planned to go to the Unicorns' party with Amy and the others. She was very interested in seeing the projects the other kids had been working on for the past couple of weeks. Brooke Dennis was going to play some really good tapes and even Caroline Pearce's art collection promised to be interesting. *The Sixers* staff was also going to hand out their special edition on Santa Doran current events. They were saving the scrapbook until lunchtime tomorrow, when they were going to present it in front of the whole school.

But the more Elizabeth had thought about poor

Arthur, having to put up with everybody fawning over him at the party, the more miserable she felt. And by the time she got home from school, she had decided not to go to the party at all.

"Are you sure you're not coming down with something, dear?" Mrs. Wakefield asked worriedly, when Elizabeth told her that she'd decided to stay home.

"No," Elizabeth told her mother. "I'm not sick. I'm just . . . well, I just wish Arthur didn't hold me responsible for telling people who he is. I could see all week how unhappy he was. And I can't go to the party and act like I'm having fun when I know that *he's* not having fun. The party is exactly the kind of thing he *hates*—everybody making a big fuss over him because he's royalty."

Mrs. Wakefield nodded that she understood, and gave Elizabeth an extra-warm hug. But when Jessica found out, she frowned.

"You *can't* stay home, Lizzie," she said. "It's going to be the best party of the year!"

Elizabeth saw that Jessica was already dressed in her pink-and-white party dress. Over the dress she was wearing the little Santa Doran lace apron she had made from a picture in Elizabeth's book, and she had pinned on a ruffled headpiece decorated with pink-and-white ribbons. She looked just like a Santa Doran girl.

Elizabeth managed a smile. "That's OK, Jess," she said. "I just don't feel like going, that's all." For a minute, she was more than half-tempted to tell her twin that *she* was the one who was supposed to walk to the party with Arthur. But that wasn't exactly fair. It hadn't been Jessica's fault that Arthur had gotten so upset. Jessica might be a little impulsive, but she was intensely loyal to her sister. If she knew that Elizabeth was supposed to go with Arthur, she might refuse to go herself.

Elizabeth turned away, gesturing toward a box on the bed. "Anyway, I've got all this stuff to finish putting in Arthur's scrapbook," she said. "We're supposed to give it to him tomorrow, and if I don't work on it, it won't get done."

Jessica sighed and turned toward the door. "Well," she said, "whatever's bothering you, I hope you feel better soon."

"So do I," Elizabeth said under her breath. "So do I." But she wasn't at all sure how soon that would be.

At the party, Jessica wasn't feeling much better than Elizabeth. All week, she had imagined how it would be to walk onto Ellen's elegant patio—

hundreds of lights twinkling, Brooke's Santa Doran melodies filling the air—on the arm of Prince Arthur, the handsomest prince she had ever seen. All the Unicorns would turn and stare, especially Lila and Janet, who were bound to be green with envy. Everyone else would bow as the royal couple walked past on their way to the throne (Ellen's grandfather's carved walnut chair), where Arthur would sit in dignified splendor while she stood beside him. And they would dance together, as everybody looked on, and Arthur would whisper in her ear that she was more beautiful than any princess. It was going to be a *fabulous* evening— the most beautiful, most wonderful evening of her life.

But now Jessica had to admit that things hadn't gotten off to a very good start. It was really sad to think of her sister staying at home, while she was having fun at a gala party. Somehow, it didn't seem right.

And the other problem was Arthur. Jessica had been sure she'd feel like a princess, dancing at the party with the most handsome prince in the world. But even though her prince *was* handsome—and at the Unicorns' request, he was even wearing his dark blue Royal Navy uniform with medallions plastered all over the front—he wasn't acting at all princely.

In fact, Arthur was acting more like a *frog* than a prince. He was glum and mopey. Oh, he was courteous enough, but he wouldn't dance with her, and he refused the refreshments the Unicorns brought him. He wouldn't even sit on the throne. Jessica thought she could understand why he might not like the throne—after all, he was used to the real thing—but she couldn't figure out why he wouldn't dance. Finally, she couldn't stand it anymore. She suspected what was wrong, but she had to know for sure.

"Arthur," she said, "what's the matter? Why won't you dance with me? And why are you so glum? Every other kid at this party would be thrilled to death to be in your shoes. It's everybody's fantasy to be a prince or a princess."

Arthur laughed shortly. "That's just it," he said. "*I* do this kind of thing all the time, so it's nothing special to me. It may be *your* fantasy to belong to a royal family, but it's every prince's dream to be just an ordinary person."

Jessica stared at him. "To be *ordinary*?"

Arthur nodded. "Yes. When I came to Sweet Valley, where nobody knew who I was, I thought it was my big chance. And if Elizabeth hadn't told, it would've come true. I could have gone to a Little League game instead of the symphony, and tried skateboarding at the beach instead of twiddling my thumbs at another old museum." He looked around despairingly. All the other kids were having fun, dancing and chattering and telling jokes, while *they* stood apart, watching. "I wanted everybody to treat me like a *friend*," Arthur said sadly. "Like a regular kid, instead of like—like a *prince!*"

Jessica closed her eyes. She was feeling absolutely rotten. Not only had she wrecked Elizabeth's week, but she seemed to have messed up Arthur's entire visit, as well. If it hadn't been for her, he might have gotten to do what *he* wanted to do, instead of what the *Unicorns* wanted him to do. He could have acted the way *he* wanted to, instead of having to act like royalty. She couldn't stand it any more. She just *had* to tell him the truth, even though it would be awful. But maybe, just maybe, he might even think it was sort of noble of her to confess. She cleared her throat.

"Um . . . Arthur," she said nervously, "do you remember last Friday, when you ran into Elizabeth in the hall and reminded her about not telling your secret?"

Arthur nodded. "Yes," he said, "I remember."

He sighed. "But maybe by then it was too late. Maybe she'd already told."

Jessica shook her head. "No," she said, looking down at her feet. "That was *me* in the hall. You . . . um, well, you didn't give me time to tell you who I was." She took a deep breath and looked back up. Arthur's eyes were widening.

"It was *you*?" he asked incredulously. And then, as the truth sank in, "It was you!"

Jessica nodded. "Yes, it was. And I . . . well, I told a couple of my friends. I didn't mean any harm," she added hastily. "I guess I just couldn't understand why anybody would want to hide the fact that he was a prince."

"So it wasn't Elizabeth's fault after all," Arthur breathed, sounding enormously relieved. A happy look came into his dark eyes.

"She would have kept your secret forever," Jessica assured him proudly. "My sister is that kind of person."

"She really *was* a friend," Arthur said, half to himself. "The kind of friend I always wanted!" He smiled buoyantly at Jessica. "Thanks, Jessica, for telling the truth." He looked around. "Where's Elizabeth? I have to talk to her!"

"She's not here," Jessica told him. "She felt so

bad about, well, about everything, that she decided not to come to the party tonight."

"Well, then," Arthur said decisively, clicking
his heels together, "I guess I'll have to go to *her*."

"You mean—you're going to leave the party?"
Jessica asked.

"Just for a little while," Arthur said. "I'll be
back." He leaned forward and grinned at Jessica.
"If anybody asks," he whispered, "just tell them
that the prince has gone on a diplomatic mission."

Ten

◇

When she heard the doorbell ring, Elizabeth put down the scrapbook and went downstairs to answer it.

"Arthur!" she exclaimed in surprise, as she opened the door. "What are *you* doing here! I thought you were at the party, with Jessica."

"Oh, Elizabeth," he burst out, "I'm so sorry! Can you ever forgive me?"

"Sorry?" Elizabeth stood back, holding the door open, and Arthur came in. "Sorry about what?" she asked, leading him into the living room, where they sat on the sofa.

"About accusing you. Your sister just told me the truth about what happened. She is the one who told people who I am." And in a moment, he had explained to her everything that Jessica had told him. "I should have realized that *you* wouldn't have betrayed me," he said, shaking his head sadly. "What happened is bad enough. But what's even worse is knowing I wasted all the time that I could have spent with my true friend." He looked at her. "With *you*, Elizabeth."

Elizabeth couldn't help smiling a little at his mournful look. "That's all right, Arthur," she said, patting his arm. "We've still got some time. We have all day tomorrow."

He looked at her, brightening. "Then you forgive me for misjudging you so?"

Elizabeth nodded. "Of course," she said instantly. "You didn't know that Jessica was involved." She laughed a little, "I was the only logical suspect."

Arthur shook his head in amazement. "I just can't believe how two people can *look* so much alike and yet be so different."

"Oh, please," Elizabeth begged, "don't be mad at Jess. She's a good person, really. It's just that sometimes she gets a little carried away with her ideas, that's all." She smiled. "You can't really blame her for wanting to get to know a prince, can you? And the Unicorns are very special to her—I'm sure she just couldn't help herself. She *had* to tell."

Arthur looked unconvinced for a moment. Then he shook his head, as if he was shaking off the thought of Jessica and the Unicorns. "Speaking of real, live princes," he said, with a glance at Elizabeth, "there's going to be a big party for my family at the Santa Doran consulate in Los Angeles, the night before we leave." He made a wry face. "I'm afraid it might be kind of boring. But since you don't have to go to these royal functions all the time, perhaps you would enjoy it." He looked at her. "Would you go with me, Elizabeth? If you were there, I'm sure I wouldn't be bored at all."

Elizabeth grinned. "Of *course* I'll go with you," she said happily, delighted that he had asked her. "And I won't be at all bored. It'll be great fun."

Arthur stood up. "I'm afraid that I have to get back to the Unicorns' party," he said. His eyes twinkled. "When you're a prince, you don't go running out on parties. It just isn't done." He hesitated. "Is there a chance that you'd go back with me?"

Elizabeth shook her head. "Thanks," she said, "but I'm busy." She smiled mysteriously. "I'm working on a very special project that *has* to be ready by lunchtime tomorrow. You see, a certain high-ranking dignitary is about to leave and . . ."

Arthur grinned self-consciously. "I see," he said.

"Well, thanks again, Elizabeth. For being such a good friend. *And* for agreeing to go to the party at the consulate with me. Now I'll *really* look forward to it."

"So will I," Elizabeth promised. And she meant it.

Since it was a school night, Jessica was home by nine-thirty. She came into Elizabeth's room.

"How was the party?" Elizabeth asked, looking up from the page of presidential campaign buttons that she was putting into Arthur's scrapbook.

"Oh, it was terrific," Jessica said. "*After* Arthur got back from talking to you, that is. He seemed a lot happier than before. We danced and ate refreshments and he even sat on his throne!"

"His *throne*?" Elizabeth held up her hand. "Don't tell me. I don't think I want to know about it."

"Anyway," Jessica said, a little apprehensively, "I guess Arthur told you what happened."

"Yes," Elizabeth said quietly. "He did." She shook her head. "You caused a lot of embarrassment for Arthur. All he wanted was to be treated like an ordinary person."

Jessica looked down. "I—I didn't really *mean* to, Lizzie. It was just that, well, it was one of those secrets that's just too good to keep! And then before I knew it, all the Unicorns had gotten into the act." She leaned forward. "I am sorry, really and truly I am. But everything turned out OK. You're not *still* mad at me, are you?"

"Of course not," Elizabeth said cheerfully. She never could stay mad at Jessica for long. "To tell the truth, I'm sort of hungry." She stood up and stretched. "Want to go downstairs with me and get some ice cream?"

Jessica shook her head. "I'm not very hungry," she said. She held up a brown paper sack. "I brought you some refreshments from the party. We had a lot left over. I'm not sure that everybody liked our Santa Doran cakes and pastries. Even if they were made by a caterer."

"If it's all the same to you, Jess," Elizabeth said, laughing, "I think I'll just stick with the ice cream. But maybe Steven will want to try them. He'll eat anything."

The two girls walked downstairs together. But Elizabeth noticed that Jessica was still rather quiet, not at all her usual bouncy self.

"Jessica," Elizabeth said, as she was getting out the ice cream, "are you still worrying about what happened last week? You don't have to worry. Arthur isn't mad at you, you know."

Jessica brightened a little. "He isn't?" she asked.

"I mean, he was awfully nice to me when he came back to the party, after he'd talked to you. But I thought that was just because he was happy to find out that you weren't responsible for what happened." She frowned. "I'd hate to have a prince mad at me."

Elizabeth shook her head. "He's not mad. He's just a little sad, that's all. I'm sure he wishes he'd had more time to make friends—and of course, everybody was half-afraid of him, once they found out he was a prince. People treated him so differently."

Jessica sighed. "Yes, I know," she said. "I really messed things up for him. I wish I could find a way to . . ." Her voice trailed off and she got a speculative look in her eyes.

Elizabeth stopped dishing out the ice cream and stared at her twin, beginning to feel suspicious. "Jessica Wakefield," she demanded, "what are you thinking?"

"Oh, nothing." Jessica replied innocently. "Nothing at all." She smiled an angelic smile. "Actually, I think I'll have some of that ice cream after all."

Eleven

"I think," Amy said, as she sat down next to Elizabeth in the cafeteria, "that there's something funny going on around here."

"Something funny?" Elizabeth asked, buttering her roll.

Amy pushed her blond hair out of her eyes and sat down. "Arthur was in the lunch line ahead of me a minute ago, and he was actually carrying his *own* tray. And not only that, but Lila Fowler and Ellen Riteman cut in line, right in front of him!"

Elizabeth laughed. "That *is* funny," she agreed. "Especially after the last few days, when the Unicorns have been waiting on him hand and foot." She paused, thinking. "Come to think of it, this morning in homeroom, I saw Jerry McAllister throw a spitball at him. And when he opened his desk, there was a rubber frog inside.''

Jessica put down her tray. "Is anybody sitting here?" she asked, pulling out an empty chair.

"No," Elizabeth said. She was staring at her sister. "Jess," she said in a stern voice, "have you been up to any monkey business this morning?"

"Monkey business?" Jessica asked innocently. "Why, Elizabeth Wakefield, you can't possibly think that I would—"

"Is there room for one more?" Arthur interrupted, coming up with his tray.

"Sure," Elizabeth said. "Plenty of room."

Arthur pulled out a chair and sat down. He was staring at a bowl of green Jell-O on his tray.

"What's the matter?" Amy asked. "Don't you like Jell-O?"

Arthur shook his head. "It's not that," he said. "It's just that I was getting a brownie for dessert and Lois Waller snatched it right out of my hand. All that was left was this green Jell-O."

"Mm-m-m-m," Elizabeth said, with a glance at Jessica. Her twin's face was red and she looked as if she were about to burst. "Has anything else odd happened to you this morning?"

Arthur picked up his sandwich. "Well, as a matter of fact, it has," he said, as if he were still trying to sort things out. "I was walking down the hall between second and third period, and Charlie Cashman came tearing around the corner and nearly knocked me down." He looked up. "And he didn't say 'Pardon me, Your Highness,' the way he did when he bumped into me at recess yesterday. He didn't even say 'Excuse me.' "

Jessica spluttered into her milk. "What did he say?" she asked.

"He said, 'Why don't you look where you're going, you idiot.' "

Jessica burst into giggles, and Elizabeth and Amy joined her. In a moment the giggles had turned into peals of laughter.

Arthur looked from one to the other. "I think," he said mildly, "that something is going on here that I don't know about."

"You're right, Your Highness—I mean, Arthur," Amy said, wiping her eyes. "It certainly is."

Elizabeth pointed at her sister. "And I think you have Jessica to thank for it," she said.

Arthur raised his eyebrows. "Jessica?"

"Well, you *said* you wanted to be treated like an ordinary kid," Jessica said. She gave him a smug look as a couple of kids pushed past the table, jostling Arthur. "So I spread the word. How do you like it?"

Arthur shook his head, grinning. "So *this* is what it's like to be a regular kid," he said, with a glance at the bowl of green Jell-O.

"Right," the girls chorused.

"How do you like it?" Jessica repeated anxiously.

Arthur leaned forward. "Jessica," he said, "isn't that Janet Howell over there, waving at you?"

As Jessica turned to look, Arthur quickly traded his bowl of Jell-O for the brownie on Jessica's tray. And then he sat back in his chair, a big smile on his face. "I *love* being a regular kid," he said blissfully.

Amy continued to laugh as she stood up. "Excuse me," she said, with a glance at Elizabeth. "But I have an errand to do. See you in a few minutes."

When Amy had gone, Arthur said, "You know, I've been thinking." He glanced at Elizabeth. "About that party, at the consulate."

Elizabeth nodded, guessing what Arthur had in mind. "I think that's a great idea, Arthur."

"Well, then," Arthur said, turning to Jess, "would you like to go to the party with Elizabeth and me at the Santa Doran consulate this weekend?"

"Oh, Arthur!" Jessica squealed, "I'd *love* to! Oh, thank you!"

At that moment, Mr. Clark, the principal, walked into the lunchroom. Amy was with him, and she was carrying a package. Mr. Clark clapped for everybody's attention, and then he said, "We have a very special presentation to make this afternoon. Would our exchange student, Arthur Castle, please come forward, and also Elizabeth Wakefield, editor of *The Sweet Valley Sixers*?"

Together, Elizabeth and Arthur went up front. And then Mr. Clark and Elizabeth presented Arthur with the scrapbook *The Sixers* staff had made for him, on behalf of the entire sixth grade.

"I'm really honored," Arthur said, turning the pages happily. "To think that you went to all this work, just for me! It's great! Thank you!" He turned to the kids in the lunchroom. "And thank you to everybody, for making my visit such a memorable—"

But Arthur never got to finish his sentence. At that moment, Jerry McAllister stood up in the back of the room. "Hey, Prince," he yelled, "look out!" And he sailed a paper airplane right into the middle of Arthur's chest. For a second, Arthur just stood there, stunned. And then he burst into laughter. And the rest of the kids all began to laugh, too.

The evening at the Santa Doran consulate was unlike any other evening of Elizabeth's life. She and Jessica had spent hours getting ready. They were wearing look-alike white ruffled dresses and carrying the lovely orchid-and-rose bouquets that Arthur had given them. And Arthur looked more handsome and regal than ever before, in a royal blue uniform with a red stripe down the trouser legs and a red satin sash loaded with gold and silver medals across his chest. He had called for them in a long black limousine driven by a uniformed chauffeur, and Steven's mouth had dropped open as he watched the prince escort his sisters to the car. Elizabeth couldn't resist giving her brother a broad wink and a wave as she climbed into the car and they sped off.

At the party, the girls made a grand entrance with Arthur, one on each arm, down a wide red-carpeted staircase lit with twinkling lights. At the foot of the staircase, they were introduced to King Armand and Queen Stephanie, and both Jessica and Elizabeth got to give the curtsies they had been practicing.

King Armand smiled down at them. Elizabeth saw that he had dark eyes, like his son's, and the same almost-shy smile. "It is good to meet the young woman who has been so kind to my son," he said. "The Queen and I are grateful that you showed him so much wonderful American hospitality." He gave her a low bow.

Elizabeth colored and her heart beat fast. Then she smiled as Arthur leaned over to his father. "You should see her throw a Frisbee, Father," he said, in a loud whisper, and they all laughed.

Arthur joined the receiving line with his father and mother, and Elizabeth and Jessica went to stand in the corner where they could see everything that was going on. A waiter in black tie and tails brought them each a cup of punch and a small plate of delicate pastries.

Jessica frowned when she looked at the pastries. "Oh," she said, "is *that* what they were supposed to look like." She wrinkled her nose. "No wonder we had so many leftovers."

Elizabeth laughed and nudged her sister. "Look over there," she whispered. "It's the Governor of California!"

"And isn't that Monica Stewart, standing beside him?" Jessica asked, her eyes wide. "I *loved* her new movie." She looked around. "But I don't see

Johnny Buck anywhere," she added, in a disappointed voice.

"Maybe he's on tour," Elizabeth said. "Look, would you believe it? There's Kirk Kellerman! Doesn't he look *handsome*?"

"You know," Jessica said, with a happy sigh, sipping her punch, "I'm so glad things happened the way they did. With you and Arthur, I mean. Maybe you were both a little unhappy for a few days, but if it hadn't been for that, we might not be here at this fabulous party tonight."

Elizabeth thought for a minute. "I guess you're right, Jessica, although I'm not sure that *all* that grief was necessary."

"And look at Arthur," Jessica said, continuing. "Doesn't he look wonderful? He looks exactly like a prince, if you ask me."

At that moment, Arthur was standing between his father and his mother, greeting people. In his regal uniform, straight and tall, he *did* look exactly like a prince, Elizabeth thought.

She laughed a little. "Yes," she said, "I have to agree. Arthur may have wanted to be a normal kid. But the truth is, he makes a great prince."

"Then did he bring you *home* in the limousine?" Amy asked eagerly. Elizabeth, Jessica, Amy, and

Mary were all walking home together after school on Monday. Jessica had just finished describing the wonderful party at the consulate, and the royal way that Prince Arthur had treated them.

"Yes," Elizabeth said. She giggled a little. "But we had to stop at Casey's before we went home. Arthur said he just couldn't leave Sweet Valley without having one last chocolate milk shake."

"Yeah, you should have seen the people at the ice cream parlor *gawking* at us," Jessica said. "Arthur was dressed up in his best uniform, with all his medals on a sash across his chest, and we were still carrying our orchids and roses. And there was this long black limousine parked out in front, with a chauffeur and everything." She rolled her eyes. "It was absolutely *incredible*. I'm sure everybody was impressed out of their minds."

"Right," Elizabeth laughed. "With Arthur in his costume and us with our bouquets, they probably thought we were coming back from a Halloween party!"

Jessica sighed. "It's just too bad that it's all over and he's on his way back to Santa Dora," she said regretfully. "What'll we do for excitement now that our favorite prince is gone? Homeroom is going to be awfully dull."

Amy sighed. "Oh, well. It was great while it lasted."

"Actually," Mary reminded them, "there *is* a new face in homeroom."

Amy nodded. "Sandra Ferris, you mean. She's sitting next to me."

"She's not exactly a new face," Elizabeth said thoughtfully. "We used to be friends back in elementary school. Then we both got interested in different things, and we hardly ever got to see each other anymore. I sort of lost track of her. I think she even went to a different school for a year."

Jessica sniffed. "You were friends with Sandra Ferris? She's one of the plainest-looking girls I've ever seen. Lila was saying how weird she looked, with her hair pulled straight back that way and the ends all split and frizzy. And she doesn't seem to know what to do with her *feet*—they keep sticking out into the aisle." She tossed her blond hair. "If we had a competition for Miss Plain Jane of the Sixth Grade, Sandra Ferris would win, hands down."

Amy giggled. "I have to admit," she said, "Sandra isn't likely to be nominated prom queen."

"No kidding," Mary put in. "And she isn't very nice, either. I tried to talk to her, but she just muttered something. She wouldn't even *look* at me! She kept her eyes on the floor all the time I was trying to be nice to her."

Listening to her sister and their friends, Elizabeth was beginning to feel uncomfortable, although she wasn't exactly sure why. They were certainly right about the way Sandra Ferris *looked*. Elizabeth had been busy with a special assignment this morning, so she hadn't had a chance to talk to Sandra, or even say hi to her. But she had seen her from across the room, sitting with her shoulders all hunched over and a book pulled up close to her face. It looked as if she was trying to hide herself from the curious gaze of the other sixth graders. Elizabeth wasn't sure whether it was because Sandra didn't like the other kids or whether she was afraid of them.

Jessica sighed. "Well," she said, with a dreamy, far-away look in her eyes, "it wasn't hard to tell that Arthur Castle was different when he first arrived. With those dark eyes and curly hair, you knew just by looking at him that he was somebody special." She made a face. "And you can tell by looking at Sandra Ferris that she's an ugly duckling and she's going to stay that way her whole, entire life."

Mary and Amy agreed loudly with Jessica. And even Elizabeth had to admit that it certainly looked as if her sister was right.

Is Sandra Ferris going to be an ugly duckling forever? Find out in Sweet Valley Twins #31, JESSICA'S BAD IDEA.

☐ **BEST FRIENDS #1** ....15655-1/$2.99
☐ **TEACHER'S PET #2** ....15656-X/$2.99
☐ **THE HAUNTED HOUSE #3** ....15657-8/$2.99
☐ **CHOOSING SIDES #4** ....15658-6/$2.99
☐ **SNEAKING OUT #5** ....15659-4/$2.99
☐ **THE NEW GIRL #6** ....15660-8/$2.95
☐ **THREE'S A CROWD #7** ....15661-6/$2.99
☐ **FIRST PLACE #8** ....15662-4/$2.99
☐ **AGAINST THE RULES #9** ....15676-4/$2.99
☐ **ONE OF THE GANG #10** ....15677-2/$2.75
☐ **BURIED TREASURE #11** ....15692-6/$2.95
☐ **KEEPING SECRETS #12** ....15702-7/$2.99
☐ **STRETCHING THE TRUTH #13** ....15645-3/$2.95
☐ **TUG OF WAR #14** ....15663-2/$2.99
☐ **THE OLDER BOY #15** ....15664-0/$2.99
☐ **SECOND BEST #16** ....15665-9/$2.75
☐ **BOYS AGAINST GIRLS #17** ....15666-7/$2.99
☐ **CENTER OF ATTENTION #18** ....15668-3/$2.75
☐ **THE BULLY #19** ....15667-5/$2.99
☐ **PLAYING HOOKY #20** ....15606-3/$2.99
☐ **LEFT BEHIND #21** ....15609-8/$2.75
☐ **OUT OF PLACE #22** ....15628-4/$2.75
☐ **CLAIM TO FAME #23** ....15624-1/$2.75
☐ **JUMPING TO CONCLUSIONS #24** ....15635-7/$2.75
☐ **STANDING OUT #25** ....15653-5/$2.75
☐ **TAKING CHARGE #26** ....15669-1/$2.75

Buy them at your local bookstore or use this handy page for ordering:

Bantam Books, Dept. SVT3, 414 East Golf Road, Des Plaines, IL 60016

Please send me the items I have checked above. I am enclosing $_____
(please add $2.50 to cover postage and handling). Send check or money
order, no cash or C.O.D.s please.

Mr/Ms _____

Address _____

City/State_____ Zip_____

Please allow four to six weeks for delivery.   SVT3-9/91
Prices and availability subject to change without notice.

☐	15681-0	**TEAMWORK #27**	**$2.75**
☐	15688-8	**APRIL FOOL! #28**	**$2.75**
☐	15695-0	**JESSICA AND THE BRAT ATTACK #29**	**$2.75**
☐	15715-9	**PRINCESS ELIZABETH #30**	**$2.95**
☐	15727-2	**JESSICA'S BAD IDEA #31**	**$2.75**
☐	15747-7	**JESSICA ON STAGE #32**	**$2.99**
☐	15753-1	**ELIZABETH'S NEW HERO #33**	**$2.99**
☐	15766-3	**JESSICA, THE ROCK STAR #34**	**$2.99**
☐	15772-8	**AMY'S PEN PAL #35**	**$2.95**
☐	15778-7	**MARY IS MISSING #36**	**$2.99**
☐	15779-5	**THE WAR BETWEEN THE TWINS #37**	**$2.99**
☐	15789-2	**LOIS STRIKES BACK #38**	**$2.99**
☐	15798-1	**JESSICA AND THE MONEY MIX-UP #39**	**$2.95**
☐	15806-6	**DANNY MEANS TROUBLE #40**	**$2.99**
☐	15810-4	**THE TWINS GET CAUGHT #41**	**$2.99**
☐	15824-4	**JESSICA'S SECRET #42**	**$2.95**
☐	15835-X	**ELIZABETH'S FIRST KISS #43**	**$2.95**
☐	15837-6	**AMY MOVES IN #44**	**$2.95**
☐	15843-0	**LUCY TAKES THE REINS #45**	**$2.99**
☐	15849-X	**MADEMOISELLE JESSICA #46**	**$2.95**
☐	15869-4	**JESSICA'S NEW LOOK #47**	**$2.95**
☐	15880-5	**MANDY MILLER FIGHTS BACK #48**	**$2.99**
☐	15899-6	**THE TWINS' LITTLE SISTER #49**	**$2.99**
☐	15911-9	**JESSICA AND THE SECRET STAR #50**	**$2.99**

Bantam Books, Dept. SVT5, 414 East Golf Road, Des Plaines, IL 60016

Please send me the items I have checked above. I am enclosing $_____
(please add $2.50 to cover postage and handling). Send check or money
order, no cash or C.O.D.s please.

Mr/Ms _____

Address _____

City/State _____ Zip _____

Please allow four to six weeks for delivery.
Prices and availability subject to change without notice.

SVT5-9/91